THE NEWSPAPER PIRATES

Written by j wallace skelton

Illustrated by Ketch Wehr

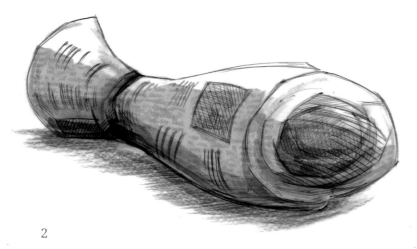

I'm Anthony Bartholomew, and I'm the King of the Newspaper Pirates.
I have a pirate ship, a pirate sword, and a pirate hat (made of newspaper of course).
Thanks to me, my Papa gets his newspaper every morning.

I used to be plain Anthony Bartholomew and my Papa's newspaper used to get taken by pirates. All the time.
Should I tell you how I made the other pirates stop taking his paper?

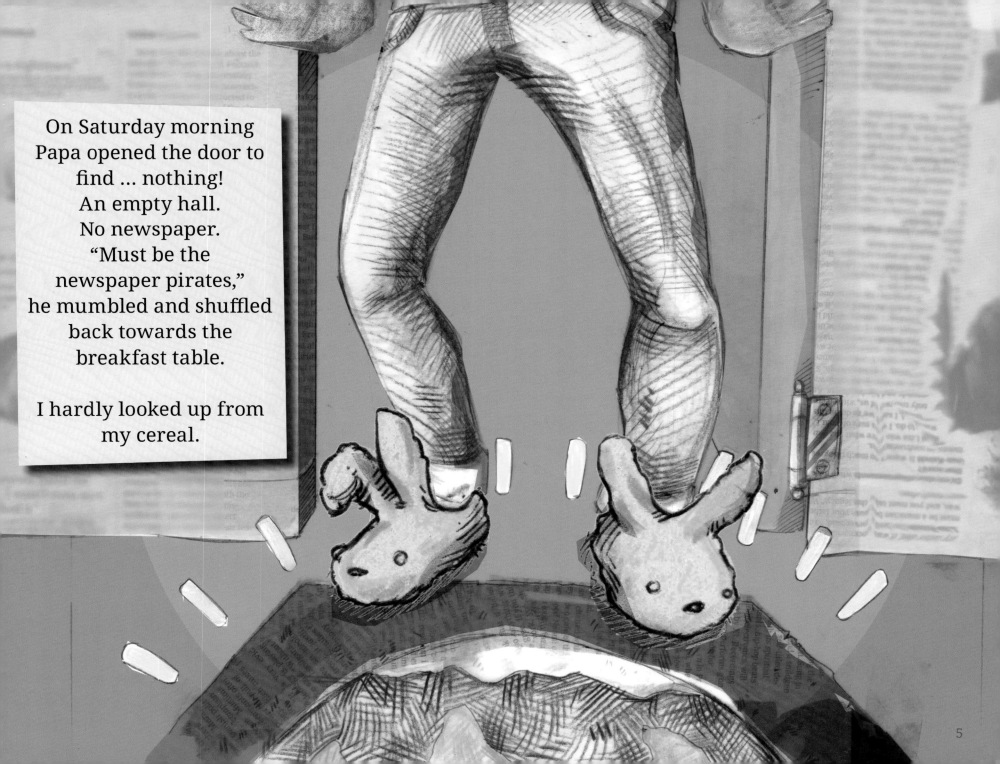

On Saturday morning Papa opened the door to find ... nothing!
An empty hall.
No newspaper.
"Must be the newspaper pirates," he mumbled and shuffled back towards the breakfast table.

I hardly looked up from my cereal.

On Sunday, the newspaper pirates struck again.
This time I was mad – no newspaper meant no comics!
Papa called the newspaper and had them deliver another one.
But everyone knows, comics are supposed to be read at breakfast.

On Monday, I get home first. Papa and Abba are both still at work.
I'm supposed to go right upstairs to the Martins' and visit with them,
but I don't always go right away.
I decided look around for the newspaper pirates.

I started in the laundry room. Almost everyone goes there,
so I figured that the pirates must do laundry there too.
I looked for eye patches, spotted handkerchiefs, or pirate flags.
But all the laundry in the driers just looked like laundry.

Upstairs, I knocked on the Martins' door.
They're way older than my parents, and I didn't want to scare them,
so I didn't say the word "pirate". I just asked if they had seen
any extra newspapers anywhere. They hadn't.

Mrs. Martin poured me a glass of milk and asked if I needed the newspaper for a school project. "Yes?" I said, eating apple slices and cheese. "Then perhaps Mr. Martin can take you down to the recycling room after your snack."

The recycling room is in the basement. It's stacked high with newspapers and cardboard and in the corner there's a REALLY big box. Mr. Martin says he'll help me take it upstairs. When we move the box, I think I see a sword.

It is a sword! It has a gold plastic blade and handle.
It must belong to the pirates – perhaps they upgraded?
I grab it quick. Mr. Martin thinks I want to play with it, but really,
I want to examine it for clues.

I hide the sword in my bedroom when we get upstairs. I'm supposed to work on my homework, but really I'm thinking about the newspaper pirates (and what I can do with my box). I think I'll make it into a pirate ship.

The pirates must have taken some time off!
On Tuesday, Wednesday and Thursday the paper arrived on
our doorstep exactly as it should, by breakfast time.

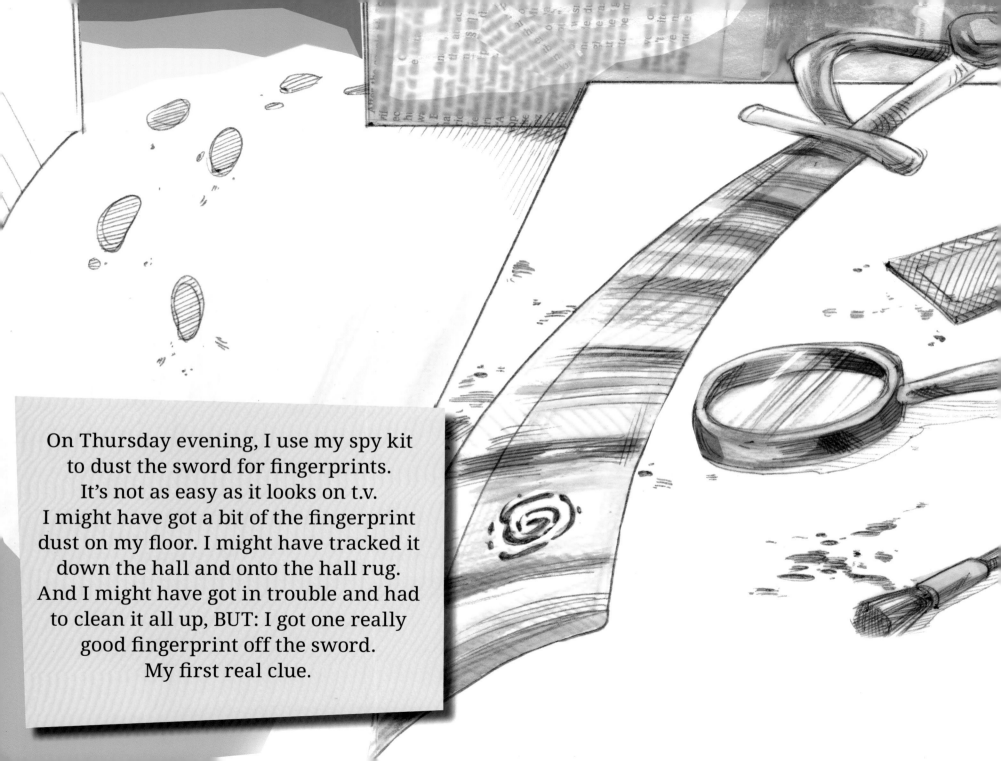

On Thursday evening, I use my spy kit
to dust the sword for fingerprints.
It's not as easy as it looks on t.v.
I might have got a bit of the fingerprint
dust on my floor. I might have tracked it
down the hall and onto the hall rug.
And I might have got in trouble and had
to clean it all up, BUT: I got one really
good fingerprint off the sword.
My first real clue.

That night, in bed, Abba read me books and tucked me in. I thought about the fingerprint. I thought about going through our building and dusting every doorknob until I found a match, but I might get caught.
Also, I'm not sure I have enough powder.

On Friday morning,
I went to get the newspaper.
I opened the door partly hoping it was
there, and partly hoping it was missing.
The newspaper pirates had struck again!
Papa said it wasn't kind to him to seem
so pleased that his paper was missing.
I tried looking glummer.

On Friday, when I got home from school, I'd thought of a new way to catch the newspaper pirates. As soon as I got home, I went to the recycling room and grabbed a newspaper.

I went to the bathroom and got a long piece of dental floss.
I tied one end of the dental floss to the elastic holding the newspaper all rolled up,
and then I put the newspaper outside our door.

Inside our hallway, I got set up with a snack, some books, and a dinosaur to keep me company. I got my sword for protection. The minute the newspaper pirates tried to take the newspaper, I would feel the tug on my wrist, fling open the door, and catch them!

I waited. I waited and read.
I waited and snacked.
I waited and sang to myself.
Then I thought maybe
the singing was scaring them
off, so I waited quietly.
Sometimes, trying to catch
pirates is boring.

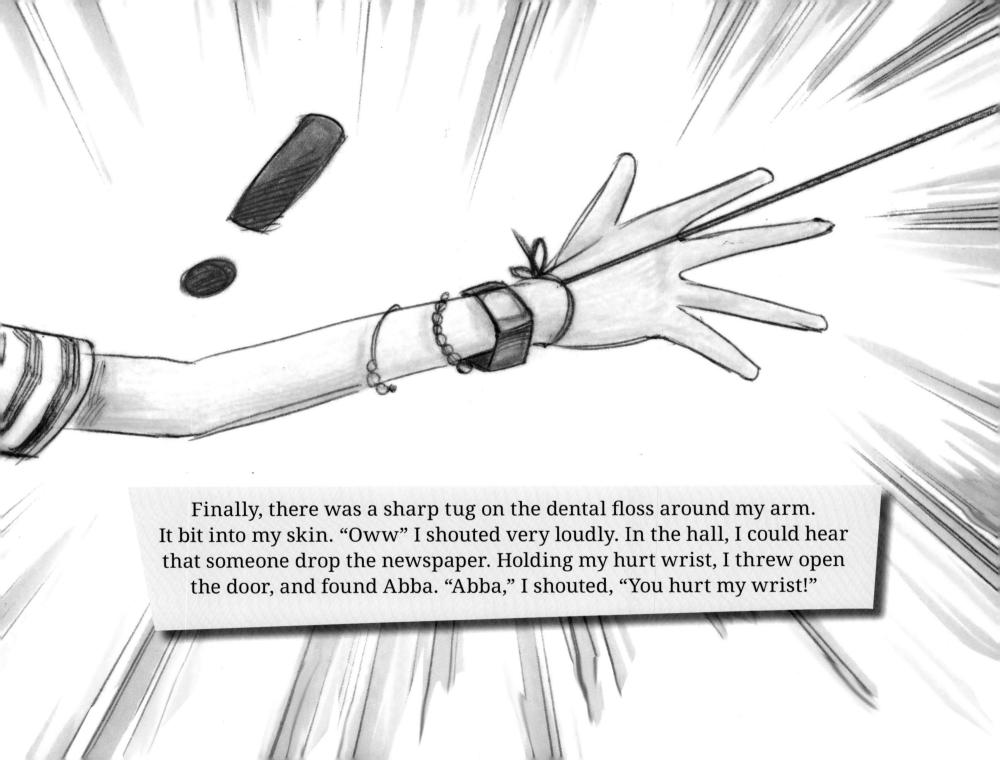

Finally, there was a sharp tug on the dental floss around my arm. It bit into my skin. "Oww" I shouted very loudly. In the hall, I could hear that someone drop the newspaper. Holding my hurt wrist, I threw open the door, and found Abba. "Abba," I shouted, "You hurt my wrist!"

Abba said he just thought this was the replacement newspaper and he didn't mean to hurt me. While Abba made dinner, I held a piece of ice to my wrist. I told him about how I was trying to solve the mystery of the Newspaper Pirates.

By the time dinner was ready, we hadn't solved the mystery,
but we had a plan. Papa came home, and over dinner we told him our plan.
Can you guess? Can you guess how I saved my Papa's newspaper
and became the King of the Newspaper Pirates?

Well, actually it was the other way round.
First I became King of the Newspaper Pirates.
We turned the box in our living room into an amazing pirate ship.
We cut portholes in the side, we made sails and put a giant pirate flag on top.

I even taped a teddy bear to the front as a figurehead.
(Papa knows a lot about boats and he said that was important).

We folded pirate hats out of newspaper.
Then, I climbed aboard my ship, and set sail across the living room.
I practiced looking tough like a pirate and brandishing
my sword in the air. Abba took pictures.

Then, we uploaded the pictures to the computer, and I picked
the fiercest one, the one where I looked like the toughest, scariest pirate
king of them all, and we used that one to make a poster. Do you know what it said?

BEWARE!

This is the port residence of the
King of the Newspaper Pirates!

Scallywags caught stealing the paper
will be forced to walk the plank
- from the eleventh floor! -
at sword point.

Landlubbers,
leave our newspaper alone!

We made the writing big and then we printed it out and taped it to our door. Our paper has never gone missing since. I know I scared them away.

I may not know who was taking our newspapers,
and I may not know whose fingerprint was on the sword, but I do know
who is King of the Newspaper Pirates. Me. Anthony Bartholomew,
and I keep the newspaper safe for my Papa every morning.

HOW TO MAKE YOUR OWN NEWSPAPER PIRATE HAT

1. Cut four inches off of the height of your newspaper (if it is 12" x 23").

2. Now it is about 19 inches high. Fantastic.

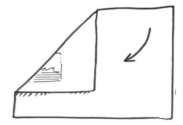

3. Fold that paper in half!

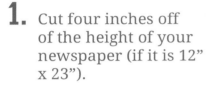

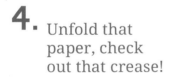

4. Unfold that paper, check out that crease!

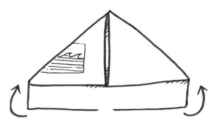

5. Fold the top corners down toward the crease.

6. Fold the first bottom flap up over your corner triangles.

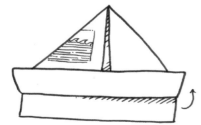

7. Flip your hat over, fold the other bottom flap up.

8. Rock that hat. Feel free to use a little tape for a more seaworthy chapeau.

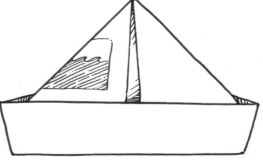